GRETA
AND THE
GIANTS

INSPIRED BY **GRETA THUNBERG'S** STAND TO SAVE THE WORLD

ZOË TUCKER   ZOE PERSICO

There was once a girl who lived at
the heart of a beautiful forest.

Her name was Greta.

One morning, things weren't quite as they should be. Greta stepped out into her garden and there, huddled together in the shadows of the trees, were all the animals of the forest.

A soft, silvery-brown wolf stepped forward, with his
tail low to the ground. "Please help us," he whispered.
"The forest is broken and we don't know where to go.
The Giants are ruining our home."

The Giants had always been there, for as long as Greta could remember, but now they were worse than ever. They were huge, lumbering oafs and they were *always* busy.

They chopped down
trees to build homes.

Then they chopped down
more trees and built bigger homes.

The houses grew into towns and the towns grew into cities.
They built factories and shops and cars and planes.
They worked all day and all night, until eventually…

There was hardly
any forest left.

But the greedy Giants had forgotten how wonderful the forest was.

They didn't see all the little birds and bugs and butterflies and bears that trembled in the shadows. And no one told them to stop because everyone was scared of them.

Everyone except Greta.

"Will you help us?" asked the wolf. Greta looked around her.
The animals looked tired, and sad. She had to help them – but how?

Then Greta had an idea.

The next morning, Greta went to the middle of the forest and waited for the Giants to come. She stood alone, holding a big sign. The sign said STOP!

She waited…

and waited...

On the first day, the Giants didn't see her, and lumbered on by.

And on the second and third too.

But on the fourth day something strange happened.

A little boy who had been watching Greta made a sign, and came and sat down next to her. He didn't say much, but Greta knew he felt like she did.

Soon more people and animals saw what they were doing and joined in too.

Before long, a huge crowd filled the forest,
stretching out to the city and the roads beyond.
They stood together and waited.

The crowd
was so huge...

. . . that the Giants were stopped in their tracks!

"Please STOP!"
Greta cried. "Your greedy behaviour is spoiling our home. You've broken the trees and trampled the flowers and now the bees and birds have flown away. These animals are homeless and our forest is dying."

After Greta had spoken, everything was silent.

But then, everyone in the crowd began to shout.

The Giants shuffled…

and fidgeted…

and stomped their feet on the ground.

They were embarrassed and a little bit sad.

You see, the Giants were so busy building, they didn't see what they were doing to the forest or the animals who lived there.

The Giants felt terrible.
"We're sorry," they said. And they promised to try harder.

So from that day on, the greedy Giants weren't so greedy!

They slowed down and learned to sit quietly.

They stopped working all the time,
and instead took up new hobbies.

They stopped chopping down trees
and learnt all about gardening
and living in the forest.

They cooked, repaired, tidied
and shared and before long…

… the forest became more beautiful than they could ever have imagined.

When Greta was not much older than you, she found out about something called climate change. This means the world is getting hotter and hotter and this is causing a lot of damage. Scientists all agree that this rising temperature is down to human activity. When we burn coal, oil and gas (called 'fossil fuels'), something called carbon dioxide is released into the air and this makes the world warm up. The polar ice is melting and sea levels are rising. Forests are being chopped down and animals are left homeless.

The Earth is already 1 degree Celsius hotter than it used to be. This has resulted in worse wildfires, storms and floods, and more than one million people living near the coast have been forced to leave their homes. If we carry on as we are, things will only get worse. Climate change is the biggest crisis humans have ever faced.

Greta knew all of this and she couldn't understand why no one was doing anything about it. So, when she was 15, she went on strike from school, sitting outside the Swedish government building and holding a sign that said, 'Strike for climate'. Over time, people stopped to join her and now, her protest has encouraged children and adults from all over the world to stand up for climate change too. Greta has spoken to politicians from many different countries, and in 2019 she was nominated for the Nobel Peace Prize.

The story you've just read has a happy ending. But in the real world, Greta is still fighting the Giants. They might not be as easy to see as they are in this book, but they are there. And some of the Giants don't want to change their ways. That's why Greta needs your help. You might think that you are too little, but Greta says:

"NO ONE IS TOO SMALL TO MAKE A DIFFERENCE."

Here are some things you can do to help Greta:

- Learn everything you can about climate change. Tell your friends and family all about what you have learned.

- Ask your parents or guardians to take you on a climate protest so you can stand up to the Giants. Ask your teacher if your class can write to or visit your MP and members of the government to ask them to stop climate change.

- Walk, run, cycle or take the bus or train instead of getting in the car or taking a plane. This means less fossil fuel is burnt.

- Try to get your family to eat less meat. Ask your parents or guardian to buy food made nearby instead of from a far-away country.

- Look after the things you have. Mend them when they are broken instead of buying new things. Share them with your friends when you've finished with them.

You might think that it won't make a difference but if we all work together, **WE CAN CHANGE THE WORLD.**

Further reading:
www.fridaysforfuture.org
www.greenpeace.org.uk
www.friendsoftheearth.uk
www.worldwildlife.org
www.campaigncc.org

By buying a copy of this book, you are making a donation of 3% of the cover price to Greenpeace UK. Greenpeace is a movement of people who are passionate about defending the natural world from destruction. Our vision is a greener, healthier and more peaceful planet, one that can sustain life for generations to come. You can find out more information about us at www.greenpeace.org.uk

GREENPEACE

For Adam, with love—Z.T.

To Mum and Dad for your continuous support and endless inspiration. —Z.P.

Text © 2019 Zoë Tucker. Illustrations © 2019 Zoe Persico.

First published in 2019 by Frances Lincoln Children's Books, an imprint of The Quarto Group.

The Old Brewery, 6 Blundell Street, London N7 9BH, United Kingdom.

T (0)20 7700 6700 F (0)20 7700 8066 **www.QuartoKnows.com**

The right of Zoë Tucker to be identified as the author and Zoe Persico to be identified as the illustrator of this work has been asserted by them in accordance with the Copyright, Designs and Patents Act, 1988 (United Kingdom).

A catalogue record for this book is available from the British Library.

ISBN 978-0-7112-5375-9

The illustrations were created digitally

Set in Adobe Garamond

Published and edited by Katie Cotton

Designed by Myrto Dimitrakoulia

Production by Laura Grandi

Manufactured in the UK by Severn on recycled FSC paper

Printed by a company certified to ISO 14001: 2015 and registered

to the European Union's Eco Management & Audit Scheme.

9 8

"No one is too small to make a difference" is a quotation from a speech given by Greta Thunberg in Katowice in Poland on December 15, 2018.

This publication is not authorized, licensed, or approved by Greta Thunberg.